The Miracle of Christmas

LARRY G. CHRISTENSEN

For all the little angels
who have gone on before us.

Chapter One

T he first time I saw him? It was ten years ago. The exact date escapes me, but the season remains vividly etched in my mind. It was late in the year, early November, I think. The trees in the valley stood barren, except for a few leaves that continued to dangle lifelessly on otherwise deserted branches. Further evidence of the season could be observed simply by gazing eastward, where an early winter storm had dusted the higher Wasatch peaks with a glistening layer of white.

At the time Dave and I were slowly winding our way through town, reluctantly driving to an appointment at Dr. Hamlin's office. I say "we," but in reality it was *I* who was dreading the encounter.

Dave tried to be positive, but I could do little more than stare out the passenger-side window of our Pontiac trying to think of happier times. I drew a blank. Had there been happier times? I was sure there had, but they were buried somewhere in the recesses of my mind. I just couldn't remember them. It had been that way for quite some time.

That's when I first saw Joshua. He was selling pencils on the sidewalk in front of Crowler's antique store. I must admit that such an occupation is not entirely uncommon in our society, nor is it as bizarre as others I've seen. I recall pausing along the wharf in San Francisco on a rather blustery day as a man, positioned upon a wooden crate, imitated a statue by standing motionless for minutes at a time. A small tin can had been strategically placed on the ground before him so passersby could reward their entertainer by tossing in a few spare coins.

Compared to such a vocation, selling pencils would appear almost genteel in nature, yet in our small town the old man stood out amidst the locals who regularly graced our streets. His ragged appearance didn't help, inspiring images of a wayward vagabond waiting to hop the next train out of town. He was dressed in a tattered blue suit and wore a pair of old leather shoes, but no socks. His shoulder-length hair was matted and his beard hadn't seen a good trimming for months.

Apparently he had no family, no real job and no place to go. With winter creeping into the valley, I wondered what he would do or where he would go when the snow and freezing weather finally hit. But my concern for the old man had its limits. I possessed few emotional reserves to expend on his sorrowful predicament. I had my own problems, so I placated my conscience by convincing myself that there must be some kind of shelter in town where he could sleep and get a hot meal.

As we drove past the corner where the old man stood, peddling his simple wares, I lowered my head and played with the buttons on my dress for lack of a better thing to do to occupy my thoughts. I guess I was practicing that old adage, "Out of sight, out of mind." Yet deep down I was hurting – hurting for the old man, hurting for my family, hurting for me.

Even now, some ten years later, my thoughts often return to that special Christmas season when the old man came into my life. I'll never forget him. Never would I want to. I grew to love Joshua beyond what my simple words are able to convey – and I still miss him terribly.

Yet to this day, even after all he meant to me, after all he taught me, it's difficult for me to speak of him. I'm never quite sure of what to say. I'm not sure

I want to say anything. The bond between us was special, something I don't readily share. But an unrelenting voice from beyond, perhaps his voice, whispers that I have no right to keep the miracle to myself, that it was not meant for me alone. And so, as feeble as my attempt may be, I obey the voice and tell the tale.

I suppose the story began when my husband and I graduated from the University of Colorado. It was then that Dave accepted a job with one of the largest computer firms on the West Coast, while I took a part-time position in a savings and loan with the intent of starting a family. The jobs, however, necessitated that we move to the Bay Area in California, and, even though we very much enjoyed the social offerings of the community, I could never seem to entirely overcome my aversion to city life. That's why the announcement of Dave's new promotion came as such a thrill. It meant the opportunity of relocating our family to a small town just north of Salt Lake City.

We initially rented a small apartment about three blocks up from the old courthouse, but within two years Dave received yet another promotion and was earning enough money for us to afford a modest four-bedroom house on the outskirts of town.

The house was more than a blessing to our family, as our children came at steady intervals. Michael was our first, arriving just one year after we moved into the apartment. Kallie came two years later, followed by Matthew. We hoped to have one more child, but for some reason, unknown to us, we were unable to conceive again. We tried anything and everything, including a fertility specialist, with no success.

Having experienced such great disappointment, we decided to give up. The heartache simply wasn't worth it. I suppose that's why it came as such a shock when, six years later, my doctor informed me that I was once again expecting a child. I'd gone in for a routine exam, having felt a little under the weather the previous few weeks. Seven months later I gave birth to a tiny premature girl. We named her Emily.

It's not that Emily was more special than the other children, but, being our baby, I guess I tended to spoil her, a transgression shared by most mothers. And as Michael, Kallie and Matthew grew, they seemed to need me less and less every day as their desire for independence increased. Perhaps Emily sensed this; it's hard to say. But she became particularly sensitive to my feelings and emotions, and we formed a bond that was inseparable.

While the older children were at school, Emily and I would play and learn together. She liked to help me bake cookies in the afternoon, and she loved to sit on my lap or lie beside me in bed while I read to her. But she would never allow me to begin reading until she had an ample supply of cold milk and vanilla wafers at her side.

Like most children, Emily enjoyed watching videos, her favorite being Winnie-the-Pooh. She adored the character Tigger, and after viewing the movie would bounce around the house for days saying "T-T-F-N, Ta-Ta for now!" She was special. She made me laugh. She filled my heart. Funny how things can change so quickly.

One day when Emily was almost five years old, I was out in the front yard, busy with what had become my annual spring ritual: planting flowers. It was a beautiful day and we had decided to stay around the house and spend some much needed quality time together as a family. I was right in the midst of my work when I suddenly eyed two small bare feet standing in front of me. I paused and looked up. There stood Emily – my precious little Emily.

"Mommy, can I have a popsicle?" she asked.

I placed my spade down into the dirt where I'd been planting flowers since early morning and tousled her beautiful blond hair. "Sure, Sweetheart, but

Mommy's kind of busy right now, so could you ask Daddy to get you one? I think he's in the house helping Michael with his homework. I'll be done in just a minute and then we'll have the rest of the day to play together, okay?"

Emily grinned that adorable little grin of hers and nodded her head. "Okay, Mommy."

I poked her bellybutton, which caused her to giggle. "Good girl."

Content, Emily turned toward the house and skipped her way to the front porch, where she called out to her father. The door opened within seconds and Emily happily disappeared into the house, whereupon I turned my attention back to my gardening.

It must have been about a half-hour later when Dave peeked his head around the screen door and nervously asked, "Honey, where's Emily?"

Even then I knew something was wrong, horribly wrong. I looked up at my husband. "Isn't she with you?" I knew she wasn't. It was a futile question, born in fear and desperation.

Dave looked at me, his eyes now filled with panic. "No . . . she's not."

Suddenly a cold chill ran down my spine. I jumped to my feet and frantically followed Dave through the side gate and into the backyard. I started to cry even before I reached the small creek that coursed its way through the back of our property. I could see Emily lying motionless, face down in the water, her tiny fingers still clutching what was left of the orange popsicle.

Dave reached the creek first and jumped in after our little girl. He carried her to the water's edge and together we placed her on her back. Her lips and skin were bluish in color. There was no sign of breath.

"Dave, do something!" I screamed, tears pouring down my face. Dave tried to remain calm as he began CPR on Emily. "Oh, Dave, how could I have let this happen? Emily, please don't die. Mommy loves you!"

Dave shook me until I awoke. "Rachel, wake up. You're having a bad dream. Wake up, Honey."

I was still screaming when I opened my eyes. Sweat and tears had soaked my pillow. Dave tried to calm me, "It's all right, Rachel. Everything's going to be all right."

I felt my husband's arms close around me, yet my body continued to tremble for some time as my heart pounded in my chest.

"You okay?" Dave asked.

It took awhile for me to answer. "I think so."

There was a pause and Dave sighed heavily. "Same nightmare?"

I nodded in between sobs. "Uh-huh." But I didn't have to answer. It was routine by now. I was being tormented by the same nightmare ever since Emily's death more than two years ago.

Dave sank back down in the bed, his head hitting the pillow like a lead weight. He was trying to be supportive, but I could tell his endurance was waning. I couldn't blame him.

He gently began to rub my back as I sat in bed, wiping tears from my eyes with the back of my hand. After I had calmed down, he said, "Maybe Dr. Hamlin is right, Rachel. Maybe it would be good for us to stop by the group and just listen to the others."

I dropped my head into my hands. "I don't know, Dave. I don't think I could handle it. I mean, everyone talking about their children dying."

"But what if it helped?" he pleaded. "We can't go on like this. We have to get on with our lives."

I laid my head on his chest and began to sob quietly. "I know, Dave. I know. But I just can't get Emily out of my mind."

Dave tenderly ran his fingers through my hair. "I know, Rachel. I miss her too. More than I thought possible," he whispered gently. "But we have three other children who are alive, who depend on us, who need our love."

Dave was right. Somehow, some way, I had to start living again. But I had no answers, no way out of this emotional pit. I was desperate, and, seeing no other options, I gazed up into his eyes and finally relented. "Okay, call Dr. Hamlin and see what time the group meets next week."

I said it, but I still didn't have much hope. After all, no amount of talking could ever bring Emily back to me, back into my life.

Chapter Two

H oney, look, there's that old man," I said, gesturing with a nod of my head.

Dave turned to me with a puzzled expression on his face. "What old man?"

I was just about to chastise him for his lack of memory when I suddenly recalled that I hadn't mentioned the old man to Dave the first time I saw him in front of Crowler's. I pointed out the window toward the park on the other side of the road. There, in the midst of the wintry elements, stood the old fellow, tossing bread crumbs to a horde of hungry pigeons swarming at his feet. They appeared to be better nourished than he was.

"I remember seeing him last week on our way to the group session," I said. "He was selling pencils on the sidewalk."

Dave briefly glanced over his left shoulder as we drove by and, shaking his head, remarked, "Kind of pathetic, huh?"

"Where do you think he's from?" I questioned. It wasn't a flippant inquiry. I sincerely wondered about the old man.

"I don't know," Dave replied, shrugging his shoulders. "I've never seen him around here before. Probably just some old bum, down on his luck."

I nodded. "I guess."

"I'm sure he'll be okay, though," Dave responded nonchalantly.

I was concerned for him, yet as we pulled in front of Dr. Hamlin's office five minutes later, my thoughts of the old man were supplanted by nervous anxiety about what was to happen next. Dave turned off the engine and looked me square in the face. "You ready?"

It was a fair question, but in my mind no person could truly ever be prepared for what was to follow, especially after the previous week. What a disaster. Dave and I had arrived a little late and the session had already begun. A young mother was recounting to the other members of the group how she had recently lost her little girl to SIDS, and I guess it just hit me too close to home.

It didn't take long before my emotions came boiling to the surface and tears welled up in my eyes. I felt so out of control that I just had to get out of there. Dave came running after me, trying to calm me, and Dr. Hamlin called after the group had dismissed, encouraging me to try again next week.

So here I was, next week already. Dave gave my hand a little squeeze of encouragement and opened the door to the office. The others had taken their seats and it appeared that Dr. Hamlin was about to start the session. As we entered he looked up over his bifocals and smiled warmly, obviously pleased I had chosen to return. I wasn't so sure that I shared his sentiments. Aware of my desire to maintain a low profile, he simply nodded to two empty chairs on the other side of the room.

As Dave and I took our seats I could feel the others watching me. It didn't bother me, though. Well, maybe a little. To be honest, maybe a *lot*. But I knew deep down they were only trying to be supportive after witnessing my near breakdown the previous week. But still, I couldn't help lowering my head and staring at the floor in order to diffuse some of the attention.

Shortly after we were seated, much to my relief, Dr. Hamlin cleared his throat as a signal that we were going to begin.

"Now if I remember right, Marilyn was about to speak to us before we concluded last week, is that correct?" questioned Dr. Hamlin, his eyes full of encouragement.

I followed his gaze to the other side of the room and there saw a beautiful young woman nodding her head. Her expression revealed fear, and she unconsciously rubbed her palms on her pant legs in a vain attempt to rid them of the sweat which had gathered. She opened her mouth as if to speak, but said nothing.

"It's okay, Marilyn," said Dr. Hamlin, leaning forward in his chair in a supportive gesture. "Take your time. We're in no hurry here."

Marilyn smiled anxiously as tears began to pour down her cheeks. I studied her face with meticulous attention. Something about her looked familiar. It was her eyes. I recognized her lamenting eyes. But where had I seen them? After a brief period of searching my memory, I swallowed hard. Of course, they were the same eyes I had gazed upon whenever I looked into a mirror ever since Emily's death. They were *my* eyes – the eyes that betray the emotions of a troubled and aching soul.

"Well, as you all know, I'm a single parent," Marilyn began, her voice trembling with emotion. "I have two children . . . " There was a brief pause and she apologetically shook her head. "I'm sorry, I mean I have one child. I had two children, but my little Tommy died two months ago from cancer."

I closed my eyes and bowed my head. At the same moment I felt Dave's hand close tightly around mine. So much suffering. How could she relive this all over again?

Marilyn started to cry aloud, but no one seemed surprised or even uncomfortable by her outward display of such private emotions. No one, that is, except for me. The two women on either side of Marilyn remained quiet, yet each, perhaps through experience, extended a kind gesture of warmth that seemed to calm her. One simply patted her knee, while the other put her arm around Marilyn and gave her a tender squeeze.

One of the men in the group removed a handkerchief from his coat pocket and it was lovingly passed down from person to person until it reached Marilyn. I say *lovingly* because, as strange as it might sound, it seemed to me that everyone who touched that hanky paused and held it in their hand for a brief moment, as if they each were giving something of themselves – strength, love, compassion, tenderness, courage. Whatever they had to offer, they gave it freely.

Dr. Hamlin nodded proudly. "You going to be okay?"

Marilyn slowly wiped her face and then raised her head. She wore an expression of relief, perhaps even triumph. Apparently she had struggled a long time just to reveal that much.

Dr. Hamlin nodded again. He then turned his attention to the entire group and said, "Everyone, as you've probably noticed, we have a new couple in our group. We didn't get a chance to formally introduce them last week, so I'd like to welcome them tonight."

My heart leaped into my throat when I realized he was talking about us. He gestured our way with his clipboard and said, "This is Dave and Rachel Andersen. They live here in town."

Dave and I looked about the room and tried to appear cordial, yet inside I was shaking. I think I was afraid of how much Dr. Hamlin planned to reveal about us . . . about Emily. I didn't know these people and I wasn't ready to share such intimate details of my life. But Dr. Hamlin ceased to speak and simply allowed the others in the group to welcome us in their own individual way. Some nodded. Some smiled. Those close by reached out to shake our hands.

After the meeting had concluded we ate cookies and chatted with a few of the couples. It was just superficial talk, though. The topics one normally covers at unfamiliar gatherings. Where do you work? How long have you lived in town? That sort of thing. No one dared delve too far into our personal feelings.

Not yet. I guess because everyone knew what lay beneath the surface. We all knew the reason for our attendance. It wasn't a secret. There wasn't a soul there that hadn't lost a child.

In my preparation for the meeting, I had learned from Dr. Hamlin that some of the children had died of a terrible illness. Others, like Emily, had suffered a tragic accident. And yet it really didn't matter. There existed only one cold, dark truth: our children were *gone*. My Emily was gone. Forever.

Chapter Three

I stared down into the kitchen sink, washing the last trace of mashed potatoes from the bowl. I had neglected to soak the dish earlier in the afternoon, allowing its smooth contents to crust and harden.

Thursday evening . . . another Thanksgiving come and gone. Holidays were the worst for me. They had always been a time of joy and celebration, but they now served only as an occasional reminder of my loss.

It was so natural to think of Emily during the holidays. The house was usually filled with an ever-increasing number of nieces and nephews, the younger of which mercilessly resembled Emily in so many ways; her facial expressions, the sound of her voice, even her mannerisms.

Such painful memories would have continued to haunt me as I stood above the sink had the doorbell not awoken me from my emotional stupor. I quickly brushed away the tears that had fallen from my eyes. Who'd be visiting this time of night, especially on a holiday, I wondered? I turned my head and called down the hall, "Kallie, would you get the door, please?"

I scrubbed the bowl a few more times, but once again the doorbell rang.

"Kallie, would you please answer the door?" I yelled out, a bit frustrated by my daughter's lack of response.

Finally, Kallie came skipping through the kitchen and into the entry hall. "Sorry, Mom."

I had progressed to drying the bowl when Kallie peeked her head around the corner with a troubled expression on her face. "Mom," she whispered, "there's some old bum at the door wanting to know if we have any food to give him."

Her announcement caught me by surprise. "What did you say?" I asked.

"There's an old guy out here asking for a handout," she declared in a tone suggesting that I personally should take care of the situation.

Mumbling under my breath at the inconvenience, I dried my hands, tossed the dishtowel onto the counter, and made my way to the front door. Once there, my heart skipped a beat. Standing on the porch was the old guy I'd seen selling pencils.

I didn't mean to stare, but it was difficult not to notice his pathetic appearance. His clothing was tattered and dirty. He wore no overcoat and shivered in the night's frigid air. His face, what little of it I could see through his untrimmed beard, was emaciated, and his hands were stiff and frostbitten. His gray hair was matted and his eyes were sunken and dark.

"Can I help you?" I asked cautiously, taking a step backward.

The old man bowed slightly, then spoke with a raspy voice. "My sincerest apologies for bothering you at this late hour, dear woman, but I . . . " He suddenly covered his mouth and coughed deeply from his chest. After pausing a moment to compose himself, he continued. "Pardon me, but as I was saying, I wonder if perhaps you might have an odd job which I could perform in exchange for a simple bite to eat?"

I swallowed and tried to collect my thoughts. What should I do? I looked around; Dave had left to run an errand and Kallie stood behind the kitchen door emphatically shaking her head "no." I looked back at the old man. My mind told me to not allow this stranger into my house, but my heart could not deny him. I gently grabbed his shoulder and carefully pulled him through the doorway. He stumbled on the threshold from his weakened condition, but I caught his arm and managed to hold him upright until he regained his balance.

"I can't think of any jobs at the moment," I said, guiding him further into the entry hall. "But we do have some leftovers from our Thanksgiving dinner."

He turned his head slowly and gazed into my eyes. "Is today Thanksgiving?"

I nodded and smiled, but my heart was aching. How sad, I thought, that this seemingly kind old fellow didn't even know it was a holiday. "Yes, it is. And we have plenty of food. I'd be more than happy to fix you something to eat," I offered.

He lifted his hand and tenderly touched my arm. "That would be most kind."

I led him toward the kitchen, but we had to stop for a moment as he once again coughed rather violently.

"Please excuse my rudeness," he apologized, "but I fear that my health is not what it once was."

I weakly smiled at him once more and patted his arm. As we turned the corner to enter the kitchen we came face to face with Kallie.

The old man paused. "And who might this beautiful young lady be?"

"This is my daughter, Kallie," I replied.

His wrinkled face brightened. "Hello, Kallie."

She was obviously flustered by the stranger's presence, but she attempted to conceal her distress. "Uh . . . hi," she answered, rolling her eyes at me.

"Please sit down here," I said, showing him to a chair at the kitchen table, "and I'll get you something to eat."

As I walked to the refrigerator I looked back at the old man and noticed him rubbing his arms to warm them. In response, I turned to my daughter and asked, "Kallie, would you please grab one of the quilts from the hall closet for me?"

Kallie had been staring at the old man, but my request brought her back from her hypnotic gaze. "Uh sure, Mom, right away," she replied, bounding down the hall.

I opened the refrigerator and perused what was available. "We have turkey, mashed potatoes and gravy, some fresh rolls and vegetables. Would that be all right?" I turned and looked at the old man; it was obvious he wasn't feeling well. "Maybe a little warm soup would be better?" I suggested.

He didn't even move. "Perhaps you are right, dear woman."

I quickly placed a pot of soup on the stove as Kallie returned to the kitchen with the quilt. Together we unfolded it and gently placed it around the old man's back and shoulders. His response surprised me. He lowered his head into his hands and began to sob quietly. I glanced at Kallie, surprised by the man's actions, yet she only shrugged her shoulders while lifting her eyebrows, apparently just as perplexed as I was. The only thing I could think to do was pat the old man on the back, which is precisely what I did for several quiet moments.

Finally, the old man cleared his throat and in a very rough voice said, "Please excuse my display of emotion, dear lady, but I have not been so kindly treated for many years."

"Don't worry," I said. "We understand."

Once the soup had warmed, I poured it into a bowl and placed it before him. Kallie, sensing the importance of our deed, raced to the drawer and brought a spoon for the old man.

"Would you like a warm drink?" asked Kallie. "We could make you some hot cocoa or something."

The old man shook his head while raising his eyes toward Kallie. "Thank you, but no, Kallie. I believe this wonderful soup shall suffice."

His hand trembled as he lifted the spoon from the bowl to his mouth. As the soothing broth ran down his throat the old man closed his eyes, savoring the taste as it warmed him. I wondered how long it had been since he last enjoyed a homemade meal.

"I hope it's not too hot?" I asked, trying to break the awkward silence.

The old man was about to put the spoon to his mouth once again, but paused upon my question, then declared, "King Solomon could not have dined so well."

Kallie and I looked at each other and grinned. King Solomon? Oh well, so the old guy was a bit eccentric. It felt good to do something for him.

A few minutes later, at my request, Kallie reluctantly returned to her homework and I sat down next to the old man to keep him company. We didn't say much at first, but he then lifted his face and spoke.

"And what is your name, my dear lady?"

"I'm Rachel . . . Rachel Andersen."

"That is a lovely name, Mrs. Andersen."

I smiled. "I was named after my grandmother. She lives on a farm in Nebraska. I used to spend summers with her when I was a child." I'm not certain why I mentioned that – just trying to make conversation, I guess. "And what's your name?"

He hesitated as if he didn't want to tell me. "I am known as . . . Joshua."

"No last name?"

"None worth mentioning, I fear," he answered.

I wanted to delve deeper. For some reason the old

man intrigued me, but I didn't press it.

When he finished the soup, he arose from the table, albeit with trembling legs and said, "Mrs. Andersen, I must thank you ever so much for this wonderful meal. Never will I be able to repay you for what you have done for me this night. I do believe you have literally saved the life of this wretched soul."

I wasn't prepared for his announcement. "You're not leaving . . . "

He pointed to the near-empty bowl with his now warmed fingers and said, "I have finished my meal which you have so graciously provided. It is now time for my departure."

I hastily stood and moved closer to him. "But where will you go? Where will you sleep?"

He shook his head. "That is not your concern."

I gently grabbed his arm. "But it *is* my concern. I can't let you go out in this weather. You're not well. You'll die out there."

He looked into my eyes. Never before had I seen eyes like his. "I do not wish you to worry about me, Mrs. Andersen. I am most certain that you have other concerns which are more pressing than those of an old man, and a stranger at that."

"Please . . . Joshua," I implored. "We have a warm bed you can use. Won't you just stay the night and get some sleep?"

Once again he shook his head, refusing my invitation. "I do not wish to disturb your family, Mrs. Andersen. It would not be right."

I pled with him. I'm not sure why, but I did. "You won't be any trouble at all. Please, Joshua, just stay the night."

He paused for the longest time, then opened his mouth to speak.

"Please," I interrupted, petitioning him one last time.

I could see his resolve weakening, and he finally relented to my request. "It is well, my gracious host. I humbly accept your offer."

Before long, Joshua, exhausted from his hunger and exposure to the cold, was sleeping soundly in a comfortable bed, perhaps for the first time in months, maybe years. I stood over him for a while. He was wheezing, but appeared to be in no danger.

I started to leave the room, but something – some power, inexplicable and yet so very real – drew me back to him. I gazed at Joshua as the light from the hallway shone on his worn and wrinkled face. I wondered about him, about his past. What had brought him to this point in his life?

I shook my head; things just didn't add up. Joshua was different. He was old and ragged, yet he possessed a dignity that defied his physical appearance. He was a complete stranger, yet I felt totally at ease in his presence. There was no fear, no trepidation about having him in my home.

I bent down and gently touched his cheek. It felt rough against the softness of my hand. Then it hit me: He looked like the old Biblical prophets I'd seen on some of the holiday television programs. The thought made me smile. I then tiptoed to the door, but before leaving I turned one last time to gaze upon my mysterious visitor. "Good night, Joshua," I whispered. "Whoever you are."

Chapter Four

D ave was somewhat surprised when I told him about Joshua that night. He couldn't fathom that I'd allow a stranger, especially a vagrant, into our home. But after meeting Joshua the following morning and observing his feeble condition, Dave also thought it best that he remain with us until his health improved.

The main obstacle to our plan, however, came from an unexpected source: Joshua himself. He simply dreaded the thought of being a burden, and it took a tireless effort on our part to persuade him to stay.

But stay he did, and for the next week we nursed him back to health. Dave even came to enjoy his company, something I didn't expect, and bought him a pair of pajamas and some underclothing as an early Christmas present.

We had Dr. Richards, one of Dave's old college

friends, come over and check on Joshua the Monday after Thanksgiving. He diagnosed a moderate case of pneumonia and prescribed an antibiotic, along with lots of chicken soup and plenty of rest. We made certain that our patient received both in generous and caring amounts.

We asked Joshua if he wanted us to move a television set into his room, but he scoffed at the idea, explaining that a daily dose of the children visiting would be all the entertainment he would need or desire. So when school let out in the afternoon and Joshua had finished his daily nap, Kallie and Matthew would hurry home to visit their elderly guest.

Daily, upon their arrival, Joshua would sit up in bed, eagerly inquiring about their school day, commenting upon each detail as if they were his own grandchildren, giving praise when deserved, and even a bit of playful scolding if he felt the situation warranted it. He enjoyed it best when they read to him, and Kallie sat for endless hours on the end of his bed, reading classics which Joshua had requested, while the old man lay in bed, eyes closed, savoring every word.

Even Dave would peek into Joshua's room at the end of his work day, asking, "How's our old friend tonight?" It seemed as if he was part of our family. We came to care for Joshua deeply, and I think he felt much the same for us. Adding to our delight, we could see that our daily regimen was working; he was slowly improving and by week's end was feeling much stronger.

It was about three weeks before Christmas that I entered Joshua's room one morning to find him in a particularly jovial mood. "You're looking better today," I remarked, placing a stack of pancakes on the nightstand to his right. "How are you feeling?"

His face beamed with delight. "Mrs. Andersen, with all my soul I wish that I could convey to you in some manner the feelings which lie within my heart. I cannot remember when I have possessed such good health and joyful spirits. You, dear lady, and your sweet family have indeed saved my life. Of that I am most certain."

I smiled and sat down beside him, feeling his forehead with the back of my hand. "Your fever is gone," I reported happily.

"Another miracle owed to you, Mrs. Andersen," he declared, patting my hand. He took the plate and placed it upon his lap, but before eating he smiled and said, "And now I think I shall return the favor in some small way to you and your family."

I guess I had a curious expression on my face.

"I realize that I have not bathed properly for some time, and I must by now be quite offensive," he continued with a smile. "I am feeling much better and would so much appreciate the opportunity to bathe and put on some clean clothing."

"Are you sure you're up to it?" I asked.

He nodded. "Quite sure, my dear Mrs. Andersen."

I stood and made my way to the door. "Well, okay. You know where the shower is," I said pointing down the hall. "You go ahead and get started and I'll put some new clothing for you here on the bed."

I did as promised and while he was in the shower I took the opportunity to change his bedding, after which I retreated to my bedroom at the other end of the house, allowing him some privacy. After hearing him reenter his room, I came back out to the kitchen to begin baking cookies: an afternoon snack for the children. The sound of someone clearing his throat caused me to look up.

I couldn't believe it. He looked like a new man. Besides being clean, Joshua had somehow managed to trim his hair as well as his beard. He looked good in his Levi pants, denim shirt and new shoes Dave had bought for him.

"I hope it does not offend you, Mrs. Andersen," he said, touching his beard and running his fingers through his combed hair, "but I found a pair of scissors in the drawer and managed to do a little trimming on myself. I felt it was much needed."

I shook my head in surprise and walked toward him, a big grin covering my face. "Offended? How could I be offended? You look wonderful, Joshua. I think you even gained a little weight."

He looked down and patted his midsection. "I do believe you are correct, Mrs. Andersen. It must have been your wonderful soup and all that homemade bread I have consumed."

I couldn't help it; I gave him a big hug. "Oh, Joshua, I'm so happy for you. I wasn't even sure you'd be alive today."

He gently grasped me by the shoulders and gazed into my eyes. "I also feared that possibility, Mrs. Andersen, but the good Lord knew what he was doing when he sent me to you, and for that I shall be eternally grateful."

My expression abruptly changed after his remark about the "good Lord," but I tried to disguise my feelings, not wanting Joshua to notice. I forced a smile and said, "And just in time, too."

He appeared bewildered. "Whatever do you mean?"

I led him into the family room. "Tonight is a very special night for our family."

Joshua's face was suddenly filled with the anticipation of a small child. "Tell me what is to happen, I beg of you."

"Well, when Dave gets home, we'll all pile into the car and head downtown to buy our Christmas tree, after which we'll bring it back here to decorate. And while we do that we're going to play Christmas music, make eggnog, the whole works. It's really a lot of fun."

He stepped toward me, a crease in his brow. "Now, Mrs. Andersen, I must not intrude on your family tradition this night. I shall gladly remain in my room while you commence your celebration of this most joyous of seasons."

"Don't even think it," I said, playfully tapping my finger on his chest. "You must know by now that we wouldn't have it any other way. You're part of our family and by tradition all family members participate."

He bowed and said, "I shall then be honored to attend."

❋

It was cold out that night and, not wanting Joshua to suffer a relapse, I suggested that he and I remain behind to ready the decorations while Dave and the kids picked out the tree. It was a beauty. Joshua's eyes lit up when we positioned it in the corner of the room and began to decorate it. No doubt it had been quite some time since Joshua had celebrated Christmas.

The kids started to laugh when I brought out the popcorn and Joshua began to eat it. "And what is so humorous?" he asked, looking up to find everyone smiling at him.

"No, silly," said Kallie. "You don't *eat* the popcorn . . . we make strands with it and put them around the tree." Her explanation complete, Kallie began to thread her needle through the popcorn to show Joshua how it was done. After stringing a few kernels, she looked up at Joshua. "See?"

Joshua curiously gazed at each of us in turn, then suddenly laughed in a deep and boisterous tone. "I am afraid that had you not intervened in time, I might have consumed all of your decorations!"

The night was magical, better than any other I could remember. I even managed to keep my emotions under control. I couldn't help but think of Emily a few times over the course of the evening, but I don't believe anyone noticed the occasional tear that fell from my eyes.

Along with decorating the tree, we played games, sang songs, ate candy, drank eggnog, all by the warmth of our fireplace. Toward the end of the night Dave got everyone's attention by asking, "Are we all ready to read the story?"

As if on cue, Matthew retrieved a small book from the bookcase and handed it to his father. Joshua looked at me and raised his eyebrows as if to question what was to happen next.

"Every year we conclude this night by reading the same story. It's one of our favorites," I answered.

The old man's face brightened. "How wonderful that you would have such a custom," he said, rubbing his hands with anticipation. "And who shall have the honor of reading this most meaningful of stories?"

Dave handed the book to Kallie. "I believe it's your turn this year, Sweetie."

Kallie opened the book, her hands slightly atremble, and began to read: "Twas the night before Christmas, and all through the house, not a creature was stirring, not even a mouse. The stockings were hung by . . . "

I looked about the room. Everyone was enjoying the story – everyone, that is, except for Joshua. For some unknown reason, as soon as Kallie began reading, the old man's shoulders appeared to slump. I'm not sure why. Perhaps he was fatigued from the long day and needed some rest.

After the excitement of the night had calmed

down, we all retired to bed. I was just about to remove my robe and slip under the covers when I noticed that the family room light was still on. I made my way down the hall to turn it off and found Joshua seated near the fire, his eyes closed.

"Everything okay?"

He looked at me with such kindness. "What a wonderful evening, Mrs. Andersen. I simply did not wish it to end. There was a peace and joy here this night that I have not felt for many years."

I sat down beside him. "It was nice, wasn't it?"

The old man smiled and nodded, "It was indeed." He paused and tenderly gazed into my eyes. "And yet, for some reason, Mrs. Andersen, I cannot help but feel that you do not share in the serenity which here abounds."

Shocked by his perceptiveness, I swallowed and looked away. "What do you mean?"

He arose and walked to the fireplace. "It is most obvious, is it not, Mrs. Andersen? Seven stockings hang here," he said, touching each of them in turn, "including the one which Kallie so thoughtfully made for me. Yet there were but six of us here this night." He turned to look at me before continuing. "Michael and Matthew share a room, while the one I now occupy remained empty before my arrival, a room filled with remembrances of a small child."

37

I lowered my head, my body trembling, but I managed to hold back the tears. Joshua made his way back to the couch and sat beside me. Taking my hands in his, he asked, "Whose stocking will remain empty this Christmas season, Mrs. Andersen? Whose room have I occupied this past week? Whose absence brings pain to your heart?"

I sat silently, tears stinging my eyes. Finally, after a long moment, I answered him, "My little daughter, Emily. She died two years ago last spring in a drowning accident. She was almost five years old."

Our guest somberly bowed his head. "I am so sorry, Mrs. Andersen," he offered. "It is only now that I understand the anguish which I have seen in your eyes. Death of a loved one, especially that of a child, brings much heartache."

"I just can't get her out of my mind, Joshua," I said, tear drops now coursing down my cheeks. "The pain won't leave."

The old man gently draped his arm around my shoulder. I expected him to speak, but he remained quiet amid my sobs. He was content to sit beside me, seemingly attempting to absorb my pain.

Finally I withdrew, a little embarrassed by my display of emotion. "I guess I'd better be getting to bed," I said, forcing a smile.

"Yes, of course. The hour has grown late." Then

as he stood, he added, "I once again express my sincerest gratitude for allowing me to share such a pleasant evening with your family. It was a night I shall never forget."

"You're welcome, Joshua. It was nice having you."

He studied my face for a long moment, then said with a tone of hope in his voice, "It is my prayer, Mrs. Andersen, that you will one day enjoy the peace you so desperately seek."

Knowing his concern to be genuine, I breathed a deep sigh, "Thank you, Joshua. That's very kind."

He turned and walked down the hall toward his room, but then suddenly stopped turned, and looked back at me. "I have a most important errand I must attend to early in the morning. I was wondering if you would be so kind as to drive me into town."

I dabbed the tears from my eyes. "An errand?" I asked, somewhat surprised.

"Something of grave importance which I have been forced to neglect due to my ill health. Something I fear that will wait no longer."

I nodded. "Sure, I'd be happy to."

"Thank you, Mrs. Andersen. Until morning then." He turned and disappeared down the hall.

I silently remained, staring into the flames below, asking myself the same questions over and over again. "Who are you, Joshua? And why are you here?"

I had no answers.

Chapter Five

Wo left the house early the following morning just as Joshua had requested. He remained silent about his mysterious errand, only saying that he needed to visit the hospital.

The landscape had changed since Joshua's arrival at our house a week earlier. A foot of white Christmas snow, eight inches in the past three days alone, had blanketed the ground, and the stores and houses were now gloriously decorated for the holiday season. Yet Joshua took little notice. His demeanor was different. He seemed anxious, even worried. As we drove through town, I glanced at him out of the corner of my eye and noticed that he was nervously tapping the fingers of his right hand on the dashboard, apparently preoccupied with something.

Uncomfortable with the awkward silence, I finally said, "A penny for your thoughts."

Oblivious to his surroundings, Joshua continued to stare out the window, his eyes squinting from the glare of the morning sun. It was as if he hadn't even heard me. But finally he turned to me and said, "I am not certain that my thoughts would be worth such an exorbitant amount, Mrs. Andersen." He vainly attempted a smile, but his expression served only to mask deeper emotions of concern and fear, but for what I didn't know.

"You okay?" I questioned. I wasn't accustomed to seeing him in such a somber mood and it bothered me.

"I will be fine, Mrs. Andersen. But, please, can we hurry?"

"Yes . . . of course," I replied, a bit surprised by his sharp tone.

"I am sorry, Mrs. Andersen," he quickly apologized. But it is of utmost importance that I arrive at the hospital as soon as possible. I hope you will forgive me."

"Don't worry," I said, touching his arm, in an attempt to calm him. "We'll be there in just a few minutes."

Shortly thereafter we pulled into the hospital parking lot. Joshua opened the door even before the car had completely stopped. "What's your hurry?" I asked, shutting the door, then trying to keep up with him.

He didn't look back. "No time to explain. Just follow me," he exhorted while waving his hand over his head in a forward motion.

And so I did, through the automatic doors of the hospital entrance, past the lobby and straight to the elevators. Once there, Joshua pressed the button and waited for what seemed an eternity for the elevator to descend. He then inched his way toward the elevator doors, anticipating them to open after he heard the bell ding and the "L" for lobby light up.

Upon entering, he hurriedly pushed the number three button on the control panel, but was then forced to wait as we made stops on the first and second floors. His foot tapped anxiously the entire time. When the doors opened on the third floor we hurried down a short hallway, made a right turn and entered a set of green doors.

The narrow room was quiet, almost foreboding, the only exception being the muffled sound of a television set in the corner. There were four beds, two on each side of the room, separated by white curtains. A dark, heavyset nurse stood at the foot of the bed nearest the entrance, writing on a chart as she checked her watch. She looked up as we entered, a smile creasing her face. "Joshua, it's so good to see you," she whispered, extending her hand. "You're looking good. You must be feeling better."

Joshua approached her and, warmly taking her hand in his, answered, "Indeed I am, Nurse Cutler. Indeed I am."

She grasped him firmly by the shoulders as a mother would her son. "We were worried about you. Thought we'd never see you again."

She turned to me as if expecting to be introduced, but Joshua's attention was occupied elsewhere as he looked toward the bed at the far end of the room. I couldn't see its occupant from where I stood.

"You must forgive my rudeness, Nurse Cutler," he apologized, turning to me. "This is Mrs. Andersen, the dear woman who nurtured me back to health."

She nodded. "Nice to meet you, but please call me Ruth. And thanks for caring for our friend here."

My smiling response slowly faded to a weak, perplexed nod. What would a man like Joshua be doing in a hospital, I wondered, and how was it that he was so well acquainted with this woman?

"How is she?" he questioned, speaking to Ruth while continuing to look with concern toward the bed.

"Not so good, I'm afraid," she answered, shaking her head sadly. "She had a very rough night. Dr. Walters was by late yesterday. Said it would probably be only a few more weeks, maybe less."

I remained with Ruth as Joshua tiptoed silently to the bed and peeked around the curtain. "I was wondering if anyone had seen my little angel today?" he playfully asked.

"Joshua!" came a weak yet high-spirited voice from behind the curtain. "You're here! You're really here!"

He made his way to the side of the bed nearest the window, gesturing for me to follow. I obeyed, situating myself on the opposite side of the bed from where Joshua stood. It was then that I finally discovered the reason for his concern: a tiny girl, about eight years of age. Her arms were raised toward the old man, beckoning him into her embrace.

They held each other for the longest time, neither wanting to let go. The little girl closed her eyes, immersing herself in the love she felt emanating from her old friend. Their relationship, I could tell, was special, perhaps even sacred.

"And how is my angel this beautiful morning?" he finally asked, withdrawing just enough to look upon the girl's face.

"I don't feel so good," she answered, her face slightly distorted from her obvious pain.

I had no doubt that she was telling the truth about her condition. Her skin was taut and pale, her eyes sunken and dark. Numerous IV tubes coursed their way from sophisticated machinery and attached to her frail, wasted arms. One look at her and it was evident she was suffering. A lump suddenly appeared in my throat as I struggled to hold back the tears.

Joshua reached up and tenderly stroked her cheek. "I know, Jenny. I know. Someday it will all go away. This I promise." He paused and gazed deeply into her eyes, communicating emotions which mere words cannot convey. Then suddenly his face brightened. "I brought someone for you to see!"

Her expression also brightened. "You did?!"

"Did I not tell you I would bring a very special person by to meet you?" he asked, turning to introduce me. "This is Mrs. Andersen, the lady I told you about over the phone. The one who has been taking care of me." Then, turning to me, "Mrs. Andersen, this is my little angel, Jennifer. She prefers to be called Jenny."

His last words were almost silent, meant for me alone, and I nodded my understanding. "Hi, Jenny. I'm very happy to meet you."

She smiled and lifted her arms as if to embrace me. Yet not being quite certain of my response, I looked to Joshua for guidance. "She likes to give hugs, too," he said with a wink.

A bit uncomfortable at first, I hesitated, but then, taken in by that adorable, innocent face I instantly fell

46

in love with her. I bent over and gently wrapped my arms around her, making sure not to squeeze too hard for fear of hurting her. But there were no such reservations on Jenny's part. She embraced me with every bit of vigor she could summon from her weakened body and said in a quiet voice, "Thanks for coming to see me, Mrs. Andersen. I don't get many visitors like the other children, mostly just Joshua."

I suppose I reacted as any mother would; tears filled my eyes and my body trembled as I held that dear little one in my arms. "Oh, Sweetheart, I'm so glad Joshua brought me by to meet you."

Finally I withdrew and Jennifer faintly smiled at me. "You're a very pretty lady, Mrs. Andersen."

"Why, thank you, Jenny. But please, call me Rachel, okay?"

She barely nodded, but seemed pleased with my request. Then she turned to Joshua. "I'm ready for the Christmas story you promised to tell me."

He sat down next to her and while carefully placing a second pillow behind her head, asked, "Are you certain you feel up to it?"

She again nodded, but even that small task seemed to require a great deal of effort.

"Very well then," said Joshua. "We shall begin our very special Christmas story."

Suddenly, though, Jenny turned toward me. "Mrs.

Andersen . . . I mean, Rachel?"

"Yes, Sweetheart?" I answered, moving closer to the bed.

"Would you like to lay next to me while Joshua tells us the story?"

Her simple request and earnest expression took me aback. I once again looked to Joshua who nodded his approval. I turned to Jenny and said, "Sure, I'd like that very much." I removed my shoes and gently lay on the bed next to her, careful not to dislodge any of her IV tubes. She nestled up against me, placing her head softly on my shoulder as I put my arm around her. I thought my heart would melt.

"Are we now ready?" Joshua asked.

Jenny looked up at me. "Are we?"

"I believe we are."

"Well, then," said Joshua as he stood and paced near the bed, "let us begin our journey back in time."

Many years ago, there lived a beautiful young woman named Mary. She and her husband, Joseph, lived in the small village of Nazareth, and at this time Mary was expecting her first child.

As Jenny listened to the story, she pressed ever closer to my body, as if she couldn't get near enough. As she did so, I gently kissed her forehead and gave her a loving squeeze to encourage her search for affection, wanting her to know that with me beside her, her search would not be in vain.

It was obvious that she had received very little love in her life and, as a mother, I knew that I could give what she so desperately yearned for. I was determined to provide it as long as I was there.

Joshua continued:

A few weeks before the baby was to be born, it was decreed by the Romans that all people in Judaea should return to the town of their ancestry, where they would be taxed.

"What's that mean?" Jenny interrupted, looking up at me.

"It means they had to pay the government money," I answered.

"Oh," was all she said, and turned back to Joshua.

A great journey lay ahead, much too far for Mary to walk, so she rode on the back of a donkey while Joseph walked ahead, guiding the animal along the path. Many days later the two weary travelers finally arrived in Bethlehem, and Joseph began the task of finding a room in which they could rest and where Mary would give birth to her child. Yet because the little village was so crowded with other travelers, Mary and Joseph could find no lodging and were forced to take refuge in a stable.

Out of the corner of my eye I could see that Jenny was enthralled by the tale. My attention was just as keen; I had heard the Christmas story before, but for some reason Joshua brought it to life, almost as if he had been there.

And during that night Mary gave birth to a little boy, whom she named Jesus, and tenderly wrapped him in swaddling clothes and laid him in a manger filled with hay.

At that same time there were shepherds abiding in the fields, keeping watch over their flocks. Suddenly an angel appeared unto them, saying, "Fear not: for, behold, I bring you good tidings of great joy, which shall be to all people. For unto you is born this day, in the city of David, a Savior, which is Christ the Lord. And this shall be a sign unto you; ye shall find the babe wrapped in swaddling clothes, lying in a manger."

Once the angel had departed the shepherds hastily descended into the village to search for this Jesus of whom the angel had spoken. They had little difficulty finding their way that night, for a new star, brighter than any other they had ever before seen, shone brilliantly from the heavens, guiding them to the stable. Upon their arrival, they reverently approached the little manger, gazed therein, and . . .

Joshua suddenly paused and looked powerfully into Jenny's eyes as if to bear witness of what he was about to say, then ended his story in a powerful yet reverent tone:

. . . And that is when they beheld the Holy Infant, the Son of God, even the Messiah.

Joshua, his eyes closing, leaned back and breathed deeply, breaking our almost hypnotic trance. Even in her weakened condition, Jenny's face was filled with wonder. "You mean they *saw* the baby Jesus? They really did?"

A solemn expression came over the old man's face. "Indeed, they did, my dear one. Indeed they did."

It was then that Jenny finally diverted her attention from Joshua to me, "Wasn't that a wonderful story, Rachel?"

Her question caught me by surprise. I had heard and seen the story dozens of times at school plays and on television programs, but wasn't certain that I truly believed it. I had thought since childhood that the tale was more of a myth. A heartwarming story to be sure, but nothing more.

But just because I thought it to be an inspiring fable, I saw no reason to destroy Jenny's hope and conviction. "Yes, Sweetheart, it was," I answered, brushing my fingers through her hair, hoping she hadn't noticed my skepticism.

Jenny turned back to Joshua. "What happened to baby Jesus after that?" she asked.

Sensing her fatigue, the old man said, "I do believe we shall have to wait for our next visit to continue our story, little one. For now, I think it is time for you to get some much needed rest."

"Oh, Joshua," she murmured.

He gently patted her hand. "I promise that I shall

return tomorrow."

She reluctantly gave in with a sigh. "Okay." She then looked at me and asked, "Will you come back too, Rachel?"

I smiled. "I sure will."

We embraced one last time, and as we did so, she turned her head and kissed me softly on the cheek, brushing my face with her long eyelashes. "I love you, Rachel," she whispered.

My heart broke instantly. "Oh, Jenny, I love you too. I really, really do."

After saying goodbye, I reluctantly withdrew, allowing Joshua and Jenny some time alone together. Ruth was still in the room when I walked to the door. "Sweet little thing, isn't she?" she said.

I pulled a tissue from my purse and wiped my eyes. "She's adorable." I paused for a moment, then asked, "Why doesn't Jenny get many visitors? Where's her family?"

"Didn't Joshua tell you?"

"Tell me what?"

"Jenny's an orphan. Has been all her life."

I must have appeared shocked.

"That's right," Ruth went on, sensing my disbelief. "Jenny's mother abandoned her just a few days after she was born. The young lady had drug problems. Jenny barely survived the birth, and she's been quite ill ever since. Poor thing's spent much of her life right here in this hospital. Had a foster family a while back, but they ended up moving to Chicago. She developed leukemia about six months ago, and she's been here for the last ten weeks."

I became curious. "How did Joshua come to meet her?"

A grin spread over Ruth's face. "It was the darndest thing. He just walked through those doors about a week after she was admitted, asking if anyone here might need some cheerin' up."

"You didn't question who he was?" I asked.

She looked at me as if I were a child, lacking understanding. "Mrs. Andersen, when anyone walks through that door asking if they can help someone, I don't ask for credentials."

I grinned at her response and said, "I think I understand." Then, shifting my gaze back to the bed where Jenny lay, I again asked, "And how did they meet?"

"He saw her sleeping one day and asked about her. When I told him, he went right over and sat down beside her and waited until she woke up. Must've been two, three hours. They hit it off right away. Since then he's been coming over every day, except when he was sick, but even then he called."

I turned to her in surprise. "I didn't know that."

"He must've phoned when you weren't home or when you were busy," she said, placing a pen in her shirt pocket.

I stared blankly at the wall before me, trying to figure when that might have been. "I guess so."

It was then that Joshua appeared from around the curtain. "Are we ready to go, Mrs. Andersen?"

I wiped the remaining moisture from my eyes and nodded. But it was a lie. What I really wanted to do was stay with Jenny, to love her, to embrace her, to tell her that everything would be all right. I desperately wanted to pick her up and take her home with me.

Joshua turned to Ruth. "My thanks, dear lady, for all you do. I shall return on the morrow. Watch over our little one."

She smiled and patted him on the arm. "You know I will."

Together we departed through the two doors, but I couldn't take my mind off Jenny. It didn't feel right to leave her, yet there was little else for me to do . . . but cry. As I thought of her, I realized just how much she reminded me of Emily, and it didn't escape me that had Emily lived, she and Jenny would be about the same age.

As that thought etched itself deeper and deeper into my soul, I cried even harder.

Chapter Six

I awoke early the following morning and was preparing breakfast and school lunches for the children when Dave walked into the kitchen.

"You're sure up early," he said, kissing me on the cheek. "I thought you'd sleep in. You didn't seem to get much rest last night."

I grabbed the orange juice from the refrigerator and placed it on the table. "Joshua wants to get an early start. He's worried about Jenny."

Dave sat down and poured his juice. "From what you told me about her condition last night, I can't say I blame him. It doesn't sound like she's doing very well."

"No, she's not," I said, shaking my head sadly.

Dave opened his mouth to speak, but then hesitated. "Uh . . . Rachel?"

Sensing the uneasiness in his voice, I glanced at him. "Dave, what is it?"

He stared down at his plate for a long moment as if trying to collect his thoughts. Then he said, "Well, it's just that . . . do you think it's such a good idea for you to go back to the hospital with Joshua today?"

Dave's question didn't surprise me. To be honest, I'd been expecting it. I knew what he was trying to say, and in a way he was right. I had lain awake during the night asking myself that very question over and over again. For there was only one sullen conclusion to any relationship with Jenny: she was going to die. And those who dared draw close to her would be enjoined to accompany her into the valley of death, the very abyss into which I had fallen when Emily died and from which I had never fully escaped.

But as I laid in bed that night, thinking of Jenny, I could still feel her struggling to draw ever closer to me, hungering for my love and affection. I felt her body still nestled against mine, her frail arms still holding me as if she feared to let me go. I felt the softness of her lips against my cheek.

She needed someone. She needed a mother's tenderness and caring. She needed *me*. Maybe I saw too much of Emily in her, I don't know. I only knew that she was a dying child and I couldn't allow her to go through what lay ahead all alone, no matter the emotional cost, no matter the depth of the fall.

But I didn't know how to answer Dave. I wanted to explain every emotion I felt in my heart, yet the words wouldn't come. We only stared at each other in silence from across the room. Yet after a moment he arose from his chair and came to my waiting arms. It was that simple. No words were necessary after all. I would never allow Jenny to die alone in that hospital, and he knew it.

For the next several weeks Joshua and I visited Jenny daily, keeping a close vigil over our precious little angel from early morning until late into the night. We tried our best to arrive before she awoke and we didn't leave until the nurse gave her a sedative so she could sleep through the night.

It wasn't long before the children began to question Joshua's and my whereabouts and the reason for our late return each night. Dave and I weren't sure if we should tell them about Jenny. I suppose we were trying to protect their emotions. But after discussing it with Joshua, we felt it the right thing to do.

Each evening thereafter, upon our arrival home, regardless of the hour, Kallie and Matthew would jump from their beds to inquire about Jenny. But after just a few days my nightly report no longer satisfied their curiosity about "the little girl" we were visiting. I initially resisted their request to see her, but later agreed. It was a while before I felt confident in my decision.

The kids' first meeting with Jenny was anything but positive. Matthew, not surprisingly, was a little shy and nervous around her. And Kallie had to rush out of the room before she broke down in tears. It nearly burst her heart to see Jenny lying there in her feeble condition, knowing she was an orphan. I guess the picture was just a bit too much.

I wasn't sure if Kallie would ever return, but the next day and every day thereafter she dropped by after school for an hour or so, usually bringing Jenny a small gift or card to brighten her day. Jenny beamed every time she received a card, and often, during the quiet moments of the day, I'd catch her looking at the cards over and over again, lip-reading the words as she ran her fingers lightly over the writing. I didn't know why until I opened a few of the cards one day when Jenny was asleep. They were all signed, "Love, your big sister, Kallie." Then I understood.

Jenny adored Kallie and relished the way she fawned over her. Kallie painted Jenny's nails, braided her hair, read to her and shared stories about her friends at school, things big sisters sometimes like to share. To anyone else, these simple acts might have gone unnoticed. But to a little girl who had been deprived of such attention and warmth her entire life, Kallie's displays of love meant the world.

Upon Kallie's arrival in the afternoon, Joshua and I would excuse ourselves and head down to the cafeteria, allowing the girls some time to themselves. On our return, Joshua and I would peek around the curtain and often find the girls giggling as if they were at a slumber party. It touched our hearts deeply to see Jenny basking in the attention and love she had always craved, yet had never received.

It was Matthew's idea to bring in a small Christmas tree for Jenny. Dave and Joshua placed it in the corner between her nightstand and the window. Kallie helped Jenny make strands of popcorn and we brought some lights and other decorations from home. Before long, Jenny's little corner of the room was fittingly decorated for the holidays, including a little stocking Kallie had made for her.

During the lunch hour our schedule was momentarily interrupted for Jenny's daily sponge bath. Initially, we were all excused for the noon washings, allowing her some privacy with the nurses. But after the first week Jenny insisted that I be the one to bathe her. It was a sign of her developing trust in me and I reveled in the opportunity to perform this labor of love.

Sadly, though, after three weeks, Jenny's health had declined to the point where our activities were limited to quiet talking and reading. Kallie still dropped by after school, but her visits were brief due to Jenny's exhaustion. Joshua sat near her bed, next to the window, resembling a worried grandfather, but Jenny always insisted that I lie beside her. As I did so, I could feel her tiny heart beating in her chest and remember being grateful that it did. I held her close, pulling her to me every few minutes, and whenever I did so, Jenny would gaze into my eyes and smile, often kissing me on the cheek. Her meaning was unmistakable.

Dave's concerns had been realized; I had fallen deeply in love with Jenny – and her with me. How could we not? It felt as if our souls were as one. I must admit that I initially attempted to control my feelings for Jenny, trying to guard against the pain that was sure to come if I got too close. I kept telling myself that Dave was right; I had to be cautious.

But after spending a few days at her side and holding her in my arms, I could no longer repress my emotions, nor did I want to. I loved Jenny more than life itself, as if she were my own daughter, my little girl. Yet the more I loved her, the greater was my sorrow. It felt as if Emily was dying all over again.

Late at night I would lie in my husband's arms, crying myself to sleep – if sleep came at all. Then each morning I would somehow summon a smile to my face and return to Jenny. But I didn't know how long I could maintain such an emotionally demanding pace. I only hoped it would be long enough.

Chapter Seven

"Good morning, Mom, morning Dad," said Kallie as she entered the kitchen, depositing her books on the counter. "What's for breakfast?"

I walked to the stove and dished up her plate. "How does toast and eggs sound, Hon?"

She smiled and plopped down in her chair. "Sounds good to me."

"Kallie, before you start eating, will you tell Joshua that breakfast is ready?" I asked, placing her food before her on the table.

"Do you want me to wake him?"

For some reason, her question alarmed me. "What do you mean, wake him?"

Kallie stole a glance at her father as if she had said something wrong. She then turned back to me. "Do you want me to wake Joshua? "He's still asleep."

"You must be mistaken, Sweetheart," I said, as if she were teasing me. "We have to leave for the hospital in ten minutes."

Kallie was spreading jam on her toast, but paused and said, "Well, I just passed his door and peeked in. He wasn't awake. It's probably because he didn't get much sleep last night."

I put the spatula down on the edge of the stove. "He didn't?" I asked with concern. "How do you know that?"

"He coughed all night, Mom. He sounded miserable, almost like when he first got here."

Concern rising in my voice, I looked over at Dave. "Honey, do you think we should call the doctor?"

Dave stood and walked toward the hall. "Now don't worry," he said, trying to calm me. "He probably had a little relapse from being outside in the cold. I'll check on him."

But deep down, I knew something must be wrong. Nothing would keep Joshua from seeing Jenny at that point unless he was terribly ill, and Dave running out from the bedroom only confirmed my fears.

"Rachel, quickly, call 911," he commanded. "Joshua's unconscious!"

❄

As the ambulance pulled into the driveway, Dave secured the front door open and went into the yard to meet the paramedics. I was seated next to Joshua on the bed, holding his hand when Dave escorted them down the hall.

He spoke softly, "Rachel, you'll have to move, Honey. They need room to work."

I didn't want to leave Joshua's side. Yet seeing the necessity of it, I surrendered to Dave's request and moved to the corner of the room. Within minutes Joshua was placed on a gurney and transported to the back of the ambulance, where a small crowd of concerned neighbors had gathered.

"Does anyone want to ride with him?" asked one of the paramedics.

Dave naturally assumed I'd want to accompany Joshua, so my plea surprised him. "Dave, will you go? I'll get the kids ready and off to school, then meet you at the hospital."

"Are you sure?" he questioned.

I nodded.

Dave gently took me by the shoulders. Through my reddened, tear-filled eyes he could see through my deception. In truth, I feared that Joshua would die in the back of that ambulance and I wasn't prepared to face that. Not then. Dave climbed into the vehicle, the door was shut and, with sirens whining, it sped down the street toward the main road leading into town.

❄

I arrived at the hospital about an hour later and, after checking with the receptionist, rushed up the stairs to the intensive care unit. Dave was pacing the hallway outside his room when I arrived.

"How is he?" I questioned, still out of breath.

"I don't know, Rachel. The doctor's with him right now." Dave pointed to a closed door. "Maybe we'll know something soon." There was a brief pause. "The kids get off to school okay?"

"Yes, but Kallie didn't want to go. She's grown quite fond of him, you know . . . thinks of Joshua as sort of a grandfather. I told her she could stay home if she wanted. I didn't think she'd get much work done worrying about him all day. Besides, Christmas vacation starts day after tomorrow."

Dave opened his mouth to speak but then nodded his agreement.

Just then the door to Joshua's room opened and out stepped a young doctor. He wore a troubled expression. "Are you his family?" he asked.

Dave and I glanced at each other and answered without hesitation, "Yes."

"He's unconscious right now," the doctor

reported. "It's hard to say what's wrong with him. Probably suffered a stroke. We'll know more after we run a few tests."

I stepped toward the door. "Can we see him?"

"Sure," he shrugged. "Maybe you being there will help."

We entered the dimly lit room and made our way to the side of the bed. IV tubes were hooked to both of Joshua's arms. An oxygen mask covered his mouth and nose, but he was breathing on his own. No respirator -- always a good sign, I convinced myself.

We had been standing there for about ten minutes, keeping a vigil over our old friend, when I felt a hand softly grasp my shoulder. I turned to see Ruth at my side. Surprisingly, she gave me a hug. "How's he doing?"

"We're still not sure," I reported. "They have to run some tests."

Dave and Ruth nodded toward each other.

"How's Jenny this morning?" I asked.

"Well, that's why I'm here . . . "

My heart sank. "Please don't tell me . . . "

"No, no," she interrupted, shaking her head. "She's okay for now. It's just that she got a little down when you and Joshua didn't show up this morning. I called your house and Kallie told me what happened. I came right up."

I turned to Dave and he read my thoughts. "Rachel, go to Jenny," he said, stroking my arm. "I'll stay with Joshua. Besides, we can't do much for him until he wakes up, and Jenny needs you."

I went, but as I made my way down the stairs to the third floor, my pace slowed. I suddenly became aware of the task which lay ahead. For the first time I would be alone with Jenny, bereft of the old man's presence. I grew nervous. I feared her illness. I feared her inevitable death. Yet even beyond those worries, notwithstanding their magnitude, loomed greater fears. The questions she was sure to ask, the questions for which I had no answers.

I quietly peeked around the curtain and looked into her face. Jenny's eyes were closed, so I walked softly to the side of the bed, searching for signs of improvement. Any evidence, any spark of hope, yet none were to be found. If anything, she had grown worse since my last visit. Her face was dark and her breathing shallow.

She sensed my presence and opened her eyes. I quickly altered my expression. "Good morning, Jenny."

Her face instantly radiated when she saw me and

she extended her arms. "Rachel." Her voice was noticeably weak.

I bent down and held her close, our embrace lasting for minutes. I decided that I would not be the one to withdraw. Jenny would have my love for as long as she desired.

At last she released her hold and wearily let her arms fall to her sides. Seemingly puzzled, she asked the question I knew would come. "Where's Joshua?"

I looked into her eyes and hesitated. What should I say? I didn't want to lie, so I settled on a softened version of the truth. "He's not feeling well, Sweetheart. So it'll just be us girls today, okay?"

I sensed her disappointment, but I could also see by her changing expression that the thought of having me all to herself for the day would serve as a satisfactory substitute in Joshua's absence.

We sat and visited, but before long I found myself once again, at her request, lying close beside her. "Would you read me a story?" she asked.

I ran my fingers through her hair. "I'd love to, Sweetheart." I gently leaned over her, opened the top drawer of her nightstand and browsed through her miniature library. "Okay, what will it be today? Cat in the Hat? Berenstain Bears? Curious George? Any of those sound good?"

"How about Winnie-the-Pooh? He's one of my

favorites," she exclaimed. "Especially Tigger. I like the way he bounces."

Unprepared for her choice, I was suddenly overcome with a rush of emotion. Without thinking, I said, "You do? That was Emily's favorite . . . " I tried to catch myself, but to no avail. Tears flowed freely from my eyes as I lowered myself back down next to Jenny.

She lovingly put her head on my shoulder and cuddled up against me. "Why are you crying, Rachel?"

"Oh, no reason, Sweetheart. Do you still want me to read to you?" I offered, attempting to alter the course of our dialogue.

But Jenny, mature beyond her years, innocently ignored my question and persisted. "Who's Emily?"

Perhaps, deep down in my heart, this is what I had feared. Maybe I knew that, somehow, she would find out about Emily, and the last thing Jenny needed was to be burdened with the knowledge of another child's death, a child very much like her.

She continued to press. "Please tell me, Rachel. Who's Emily?"

I swallowed hard and paused. I would tell her. I'm not sure why, but something told me it was the right thing to do. I reached up and softly touched her cheek. "Emily is my little girl, Jenny."

I hoped the conversation would end there, but knew it wouldn't. "Is she sick like me? Is that why you're sad?"

I shook my head as tears ran down my cheeks. "No, Sweetheart. She's not sick." I paused and bit my lip. "Emily died more than two years ago."

Jenny's face went blank and she looked away. She was thinking, piecing everything together. Her gaze again met mine as if searching the depths of my soul. "Rachel, am I going to die?"

The question I had feared the most.

I felt like crying out. I would have given my very life if only I could have told her she was going to live. But I knew there could be no deception between us. She needed to hear the truth, and then together we would face it. There was no other way.

Softly I whispered, "Yes, Sweetheart, you are."

I held her close. I so much wanted to comfort her with words of solace, yet I had none to offer. I only knew that death had claimed my Emily and that it would soon come for this precious child who lay trembling in my arms. It wasn't fair. I was angry at death. I hated death. But I had no way to fight it, no way to protect Jenny from its awful clutches. Death was the ultimate victor. Never could it be otherwise.

We lay silently in each other's arms, desperately clinging to what we had, to the little we understood,

71

both feeling helpless against such an unmerciful foe.

✻

I stayed with Jenny all that day. She dozed on and off during the afternoon. Then about seven o'clock that evening the doctor arrived and gave her a sedative so she could sleep through the night.

"You might as well go home and get some rest, Mrs. Andersen," he said. "You're going to need it. It's going to be a rough next couple of days. I'll have the nurse call you if her condition changes."

Before leaving I kissed Jenny on the cheek. "Good night, dear," I whispered. "I'll see you tomorrow." But I feared that I wouldn't.

I was exhausted, yet suddenly my thoughts turned to Joshua. I made my way up to the fifth floor and entered his room. Dave was seated at the side of the bed, reading a magazine. He appeared just as tired as I was.

Upon seeing me, he stood and gave me a long hug. "How's he doing?" I asked.

"The doctor was in about noon and said that Joshua suffered a stroke, but he was hopeful about his recovery."

I looked down at our old friend and grasped his hand. "That's nice to hear. I think we could all stand a bit of good news."

"How's Jenny?" Dave asked.

I looked at him, but said nothing. I didn't have to. My silence said it all.

His head bowed involuntarily, "How long?"

I sighed sadly. "Two days at most, probably less."

He put his arm around me. "I'm so sorry, Rachel. I wish there was more I could do."

I leaned my head on his shoulder, tears flowing from my eyes. "Me, too."

Chapter Eight

As exhausted as I was from the day's events, sleep did not come easily that night. I lay awake amidst the quiet, the room's darkness being interrupted by a solitary shaft of moonlight entering our room through a narrow opening in the curtains.

About midnight I finally surrendered to the inevitable. I slipped on my robe and made my way into the family room with the thought that a little reading might ease my mind. I sat in my favorite chair near the fireplace and surveyed the room.

The Christmas tree stood peacefully in the corner, its tiny lights glistening in the darkness. Its branches, overladen with decorations acquired through the years, sheltered an array of wrapped treasures which soon would bring joy to young and old alike. Reddish embers in the fireplace, though dying down, continued to cast a warm glow across the room. Under different circumstances, such an atmosphere would have evoked fond memories of holidays long past, and childlike anticipation of those yet to be.

But my thoughts would not leave that dear, sweet little girl who lay dying all alone in the hospital, knowing that her dreams, unlike those of other children, would certainly not be of Old Saint Nick and the wonders of yuletide. In all likelihood, she would not even see Christmas morning.

I stood and made my way to the fireplace, where I delicately touched Emily's little stocking, hypnotically staring into the flames below. I started to cry softly. "Why? Why does she have to die?" I kept asking myself.

I felt utterly helpless. So helpless that I found myself doing something I never thought imaginable: I began to pray. I'm not sure why. I'm not even sure I believed in God. So why was I praying? Perhaps there was nowhere else to turn.

I looked heavenward. "Please, dear God," I implored, "if you are there, will you help Jenny? Please don't let her die."

Then through my tears I saw it – a small gift adorned in green Christmas paper, resting on the end of the mantel. I thought it odd that I hadn't noticed it before. Perhaps Dave or one of the children had placed it there as a surprise for someone in the family. Curious about its origin, I looked closer and saw a card laying beneath the gift. Mindful not to disturb the small package, I removed the card from its envelope and read: *"To dear Mrs. Andersen, a most wonderful friend. Merry Christmas. Love, Joshua."* Even in my despair the thought of the old man warmed my heart. He had that affect on me. I lifted the gift from the mantel and held it close. Just being from Joshua made it special. I returned to my chair and opened the gift to discover that Joshua had given me a book. I turned it over and found it to be a Bible. What a strange gift, I thought. It wasn't even new. Its worn cover bore evidence that its previous owner had made good use of it.

Then I grew sad. It suddenly occurred to me that Joshua, desiring to give me a gift and having nothing else to offer, had sacrificed a possession so dear to him.

And yet, void of much personal faith, I was about to place the Bible down on the end table beside me and return to bed when, I was suddenly overcome with the urgent feeling that I should open it. I initially ignored the impression, dismissing it as the thoughts of a distraught woman. Yet once again the prompting came, even more powerfully the second time.

Not fully understanding why, yet perceiving some significance, I obeyed, and found myself opening the Bible to a page which held a bookmark. In the border, off to the side of the print, I noticed a handwritten message. I squinted to focus on the unsteady writing and read the words, *The Miracle of Christmas.*

A note of familiarity immediately struck me. I had heard those words before . . . but where? Suddenly, for some inexplicable reason, they seemed of great importance. I closed my eyes, ardently attempting to prod my memory. Then it came to me: Joshua had spoken those very words to Jenny the last time he visited her at the hospital. She was disappointed about us leaving, but Joshua had soothed her with a promise that we would return the following day and share another story with her, the story of . . . The Miracle of Christmas.

At the time when Joshua mentioned it to Jenny, I had paid little attention: it seemed unimportant. But now I grew inquisitive. What was the story about, and did it in fact have some special meaning? There was only one way to find out. I once more grasped the book in my hands, settled into place and began to read:

And it came to pass in those days, that there went out a decree from Caesar Augustus, that all the world should be taxed . . .

I read the first verse, then the next. I pored over the first page, then another. I continued to read into

the night. I could not put the book down. The last
thing I recall is my eyelids growing heavy and the
book falling lightly to my chest, when . . .

I found myself in what appeared to be a large
valley. It was nighttime and the darkness revealed a
star-filled sky, such as I had never seen before. A
cool breeze caressed my face as I looked about the
scene before me, but I saw nothing of which was
familiar. Behind me lay rolling hills sloping gently
upward from where I stood, while herds of sheep
grazed on sparse greenery. Off in the distance shone
the lights of a small town, and, not being certain of
my location, I decided to make my way toward the
village.

I had just begun my trek when a strange sound
caused me to glance back over my shoulder. There,
much to my awe, I saw three strangers riding on
horseback, descending from the hills. As they
approached I became frightened by their appearance,
for their attire inspired images of wealthy sheiks from
days long ago. One of them wore a precious gold
medallion about his neck, further evidence of his
material status.

I thought to run for my life, but the one who

wore the medallion spoke in a kind tone, immediately calming my fears. Still his question made little sense: "Would you also be following the star?"

I squinted at the man. "Star?" I asked curiously.

"Yes," he answered, pointing toward the sky. "The divine star which has guided our path these many nights."

I looked into the sky and was amazed that I hadn't noticed it before . . . a star, perhaps the brightest I had ever seen, positioned directly above the small town.

The man who spoke dismounted his horse and, asking about my destination, offered me a ride to the village. After considering a moment, I accepted his offer.

I said nothing as we traveled, content to listen to their conversation. I understood little of what they said, only that they seemed pleased that their taxing journey would soon end.

Before long we arrived at their destination: a lowly stable located on the outskirts of the town. The three men dismounted their animals and the man with whom I had ridden graciously extended his hand that I might do the same. They then removed what appeared to be precious treasures from their packs, which they carried into the stable.

Curious about their errand, I gazed further within

and, there, amidst a small gathering of animals, saw a beautiful young woman who tenderly held a small babe in her arms. Her husband protectively stood nearby. The tiny family huddled close to one another, seeking warmth from the night's chill.

Upon drawing near to them, the three men humbly bowed. Their voices were hushed and reverential. I couldn't hear their words, but the mother's response indicated her gratitude at their arrival. They then approached the infant, placed their treasures on the ground, and knelt before him as if to worship him.

Then, just as quickly as they had arrived, the three men departed, leaving me alone near the entrance to the stable. Upon seeing me, the mother's eyes grew wary and she drew a sudden breath, apparently fearful of my presence. Her husband, although gentle in demeanor, took a step toward me as a warning against any approach. I instantly obeyed his unspoken command and withdrew a step. It was obvious his wife had just given birth to the child in these most humble circumstances.

Yet, wanting to be of assistance, I removed my outer garment, which to my surprise was a tunic of some sort, and cautiously made my way toward the young mother. Understanding my affable intention, the man now smiled warmly and gestured for me to come closer. The young woman smiled, nodding acceptance of my offer.

I knelt beside her and placed my garment over her and the child. Gazing upon the infant, I noticed his crimson skin, evidence of his recent birth. The mother nestled the infant to her breast and kissed him tenderly on the forehead. She once more met my gaze, and smiled. I recognized her emotions. They were the same that I had felt after the birth of my own children – after Emily's birth.

I remained in the stable most of that night, yet the morning found me in different surroundings. How I arrived there, I don't know. I stood on a path that ran beside a small brook in the midst of a lush forest. The sky was blue and songbirds trilled a symphony high in the trees.

I followed the path until I came to a meadow, whereupon I paused, for the view which lay before me was the most glorious I had ever seen. The azure sky overhead, the wildflowers which arrayed the meadow with every imaginable color, snow-capped mountains in the distance. Never could one envision so magnificent a sight.

As I gazed out, riveted upon the majestic scene, a movement at the far side of the meadow caught my attention. There I saw a man walking towards me. As he approached, I could see that he carried a small child – a little girl – in his arms. They were both dressed in the most resplendent robes, which fluttered in the gentle breeze. As they made their way across the meadow, the man suddenly stopped, picked a wildflower from at his feet, and placed it in the little girl's hair. She whispered something to him and he responded with a smile and then kissed her tenderly on the cheek. It was obvious that they cared deeply for each other.

As they neared I was immediately overcome with unexpected emotion. I couldn't believe my eyes. I rubbed them to clear my vision, but the picture before me remained. Tears flowed uncontrollably down my face. Not the tears of sorrow and pain that I had wept these many months, but tears of an ecstasy which knows no earthly bounds. I stretched out my hands and began to call out, but suddenly the scene disappeared and I found myself back in the familiar surroundings of my family room.

But this I had learned: Joshua was right.

Chapter Nine

I 've heard it said that it's difficult to experience two dissimilar emotions at the same time. But as I awoke from the dreams of the night, I was filled with an indescribable joy, tempered by a sense of anxious urgency. The grandfather clock ticked on in the corner of the room, the multicolored lights from the Christmas tree reflected in its etched glass. It was four o'clock in the morning.

Despite the early hour, my task was certain: I had to see Jenny. I woke Dave and told him I was going to the hospital.

"Did someone call?" he asked groggily. "I didn't hear the phone ring."

"No," I whispered while slipping on my shoes. "I just feel like I should be with her."

He turned over in bed and squinted at the digital clock. "Four-ten. Will they let you see her at this hour?"

I kissed him on the cheek. "I'm afraid they have no choice."

He squeezed my hand. "You take care. I'll come down later in the morning."

Entering the hospice unit I noticed all the lights were out except for a small reading lamp on Jenny's nightstand, which shone dimly through the drawn curtain. I made my way to the foot of the bed. There was Ruth seated next to Jenny, holding her hand.

Upon hearing my footsteps, Ruth raised her head and we greeted each other with a simple nod.

I drew closer. "How is she?" I whispered.

Ruth said nothing, yet a sad shrug of her shoulders made Jenny's critical condition quite clear.

"You look exhausted," I said. "Why don't you get some rest if you can?"

She rose to her feet and stretched her back. "My shift's over in an hour or so. I'll leave instructions for the station nurse to call me at home if anything happens."

"I'll do it myself," I assured her.

She again nodded and turned back to Jenny. "Have you ever noticed?" she said, shaking her head and reaching down to stroke Jenny's cheek.

"What's that?" I asked.

"The special ones aren't with us very long, are they?"

I had never thought of it that way, but as my eyes rested on Jenny's frail body I realized Ruth was right; the very special ones aren't here that long. Perhaps, though, they don't need to be.

I sat in the chair vacated by Ruth and gently took Jenny's hand. Her breathing was shallow and faint. It was obvious she now lingered between two different worlds. Mortal life clung to her, instinctively fighting to keep her here, while eternal life beckoned from beyond. I now prayed the latter would soon triumph, and Jenny could be released from her pain and suffering. But first I had to tell her. I didn't want her leaving this world in fear.

Jenny was still sleeping when Dave arrived. "How's she doing?" he whispered.

I looked up at him and shook my head. He pulled back the curtain, stepped to the other side of the bed and sat across from me. He stared at Jenny for the longest time and then a tear fell from his eye. "She looks so much like Emily," he noticed.

"She does, doesn't she?" I sighed, a sense of warmth sweeping over me at the thought.

Dave looked into my eyes and nodded while he swallowed, attempting to control his emotions.

I met his gaze and took his hand. "It's not easy, is it?"

He wiped the wetness from his cheek and stirred in his chair. "No, it's not."

It was then that I felt a slight movement in Jenny's hand, and shortly thereafter she opened her eyes.

"Good morning, Sweetheart," I said, bending over and brushing her bangs from her face.

"Rachel," she responded weakly.

I thought Jenny was going to smile, but instead she grimaced from the pain. "Rachel, it hurts," she groaned, and as she spoke her body tensed and her hand tightened around mine.

Tears filled my eyes seeing that innocent little child suffer so. "I know, Sweetie, but pretty soon all the pain will go away."

When her discomfort had eased somewhat, she looked up at me as if begging me to help her. "Oh, Rachel," she cried. "I'm so scared." I could barely hear her words.

I held her close until her sobs subsided. Then I withdrew so that I could look her in the eyes. I paused. I knew what I wanted to say, what needed to be said. I just wasn't sure how to say it. "Jenny, listen to me," I implored. "You don't have to be afraid of death anymore."

I paused once again. How could I explain death to an eight-year-old? I'm not so sure I understood it myself. I only knew that it wasn't the monster I had thought it to be. Death had been vanquished. It now served only as a portal between two worlds.

I gazed into Jenny's eyes, willing her to believe me. "It's going to be like falling asleep, Sweetheart, nothing more than that. And when you awake you'll be in a very beautiful place. And you won't be sick or hurt anymore. You'll be happy, forever."

I glanced over at Dave, wondering how he would react to my expressions of newfound faith. Surprisingly, he smiled and nodded his encouragement. Maybe he wanted to believe just as badly as I did.

Jenny's mouth quivered as she reached up and touched my cheek. "Is that where Emily is?"

Tears rolled down my face. "Yes," I cried. "And someday I'll be with her again, and I'll hold her in my arms and tell her how much I love her."

Just then Jenny's countenance saddened. "Emily's lucky to have a family," she murmured.

How I ached for her. I never fully understood the breadth of her longing for a family until then – and suddenly I knew there was but one answer to this dilemma. I waited for a few minutes, until Jenny fell asleep, and then motioned for Dave to follow me into the hall.

When we were outside I hesitated, but summoning my courage I said, "Dave, I didn't want Jenny to hear this just yet, and I know this sounds crazy. But I . . . I want us to adopt Jenny."

Disbelief spread across Dave's face. "Adopt Jenny? You're right, that is crazy." He shook his head. "Listen, Rachel, I don't know how you came to believe what you said in there, and maybe I want to believe it too, but adopting Jenny doesn't make any sense."

I took a deep breath, then pleaded, "She's never had a family, Dave, and she wants one so very badly. Can't you see that?"

Dave went to the drinking fountain and took a long sip of water. Wiping the excess liquid from his mouth, he said, "But Rachel, Jenny's dying. What good would come of adopting her now? You'd only get hurt and I don't want to see that happen. Don't you think you've suffered enough pain?"

I walked over to him and took his hand in mine. "It's not my pain I'm worried about. It's hers. I don't want Jenny to die an orphan. I want to be her mom and for you to be her dad. We can't stop her from dying, Dave, but we *can* give her a family. That's all she wants. It's all she's ever wanted. Is that too much to ask?"

Dave bowed his head in surrender. "Is that what you really want, Rachel?"

I gently lifted his chin and captured his gaze. "I want to do this for Jenny."

"It's probably impossible anyway, with all the legal work that has to be done," he mildly argued.

"Couldn't we try?" I cajoled.

He shrugged his shoulders. "Okay," he said, heading down the hall, "I'll call John."

John P. McMillan was an attorney-friend of ours, and if there was any feasible way for us to adopt Jenny that very day, he would find it. I earnestly prayed he would.

We sat with Jenny through that morning and into the afternoon. Her morphine drip had been increased to its maximum level, causing her to doze through most of the day. As the sun set, filling the room with angular shadows, we got the bad news from John: the adoption could not possibly go through in such a short period of time.

I cried harder than I ever had in my life. Not because Jenny was dying; that I had come to accept. It still hurt terribly, but it pained me even deeper to see her leave this world with no family ties. I wanted

Larry G. Christensen

her to know that she *wasn't* alone, that she was part of us, a member of our family. But it was not to be.

❊

Jenny awoke about eight o'clock that night and, although very weak, managed to visit with us. It was then that a very distinguished older gentleman entered the room. He wore a navy pin-striped suit under an expensive-looking overcoat. I assumed he was there to visit one of the other patients, but after speaking to the nurse he quietly walked toward us.

"Excuse me for intruding, but would you be David and Rachel Andersen?"

Dave and I glanced at each other. "Yes, we're the Andersens," Dave responded

The man then turned and addressed Jenny, asking, "And would this be Jennifer?"

I was confused. Moving closer to her side I answered, "Yes. Why do you ask?"

The man shook his head in disbelief. "Then it is true." He reached out to shake my hand and look me in the eye. "Mrs. Andersen, I understand that it is your desire to adopt this child?"

I was in shock, but managed to respond, "Yes, with all my heart."

Without hesitation, the man stepped past me to

the side of the bed. He sat down and carefully took Jenny's hand in his and said in a tender voice, "Jennifer, Mr. and Mrs. Andersen have requested that they be allowed to adopt you. Do you understand what that means?"

She could barely speak, but the expression on her face revealed her understanding.

The man spoke again. "Do you also wish this?"

Jenny turned and focused on me for a long moment. Our eyes looked on one another. Our souls met. I sensed her unspoken question: was this something I really wanted to do? I smiled and nodded my answer. There wasn't anything I wanted more in my life than to have her as my daughter. She understood, as I knew she would. She then turned back to the man and beamed her delight.

He patted her hand. "I will take that as a yes."

The man stood and removed an oversized envelope from his coat pocket. Opening it, he withdrew several papers while saying, "I am Judge Clayborne, and these are the adoption papers for Jennifer. If you would just sign right here then this sweet little girl will be yours."

I instinctively covered my mouth for fear I would cry out. "You mean we can really adopt Jenny? Right here? Right now?"

Judge Clayborne looked at me and smiled. "Right

here. Right now." His tone was emphatic, as if to erase all doubt.

"And it's legal? She'll be our daughter?" I questioned as if I needed convincing.

The judge nodded solemnly. He understood the sacredness of the occasion. "She'll be your daughter. I promise."

My hand quivered as I signed the papers. I hugged the judge, then hurried over to Jenny. She was too weak to hold me, but I embraced her and together we cried. I never saw her so happy. She finally had the one thing she had always wanted . . . a family.

"Does this mean you're my mommy?" she said in a feeble whisper.

"Oh, yes, Sweetheart. I'm your mommy and you're my little girl."

Dave smiled. "And I'm your dad."

"Excuse me," interrupted the judge, "but I must be going."

I looked at him and paused. The wonder of what had just transpired suddenly struck me. "Excuse me, Judge, but how . . . ?"

He turned to me. "How did I know?" he finished for me.

I nodded.

"It was strange," he said. "I was in my study

earlier this afternoon when a bearded gentleman paid me a visit. He shared with me your desperate plight and pleaded that I help you. I refused at first, knowing the impossibility of what he asked. But he persisted with such fervor that I could not deny him."

I looked at Dave in amazement. The old man he described was Joshua – but that was impossible. He lay unconscious in a hospital bed two floors up from where we stood.

It was about midnight when Jenny's breathing became very irregular. She looked up at me and in a frail whisper asked, "Mommy, will you lay with me and hold me?" She didn't say it, but I could see in her eyes that she knew it would be the last time in this life we'd hug each other. I knew it too.

I held her close and kissed her lovingly on the cheek, lightly running my fingers through her hair. "Remember, Jenny, it's just like falling asleep. When you awake, look for Emily. She'll be waiting for you. Take her hand and go with her, and everything will be all right." I kissed her again. "Mommy loves you, Jenny. Always remember that. Tell Emily I love her, too."

A single tear trickled down her cheek when I told

her I loved her. But it wasn't borne of sadness or fear. I think she was just happy to finally have a mommy.

As she closed her eyes for the last time, a peaceful warmth came over her angelic face, and I could have sworn that right before she left this world she whispered ever so faintly, "Emily."

Chapter Ten

A s promised, I phoned Ruth shortly after Jenny's death. Together we cried when I told her the news, and she asked me to give Jenny a kiss goodbye for her. Dave and I lingered in the room for a time as I initially ignored his subtle hints that it was time to leave. I wasn't about to abandon my little girl. But as I gazed into her face, I realized it was time to say goodbye. Jenny was gone. Her frail body, ravaged by a terrible illness, lay before me. Yet she wasn't there. I could feel her absence. Freed at last from her pain and suffering, Jenny had gone to that beautiful place I saw in my dream — and Emily had come to take her there.

Dave and I left Jenny's room about one o'clock that morning. We held each other close, my head snuggled against his shoulder. Before returning home, however, we stopped by to see Joshua. I wanted to tell him about Jenny, even if he wasn't awake yet. I knew he'd understand and would want to know. But upon entering his room I saw an orderly making up the empty bed where Joshua once lay. I frantically rushed to the young man as he fitted the corner of a newly laundered sheet under the mattress.

"Where's Joshua?" I demanded.

"I'm sorry, ma'am?" he questioned, lifting his eyes to me.

"Joshua, where is he?" My tone was no less intense the second time I made the inquiry.

The orderly appeared confused. Dave stepped forward and placed his hand on the mattress. "The old man who was in this bed, do you know what happened to him?"

At that moment the station nurse entered the room. Her expression forewarned us of impending bad news. I braced myself, expecting the worst. "I'm sorry, Mrs. Andersen," she said hesitantly. "I don't know how to tell you this, but Joshua's . . . well . . . he's gone."

I peered over at Dave and shook my head in confusion. He turned to the nurse and asked the question I dared not utter. "Gone, what do you mean, gone?"

"I came in here a few hours ago to check on Joshua and he simply wasn't here. We called security; no one knows where he is. No one's seen him. He just . . . disappeared."

I was almost hysterical. "Disappeared? He was unconscious for heaven's sake. It's not like he could just get up and walk out of here!"

"I know, Mrs. Andersen," she said, trying to calm me. "We're just as upset as you are. The hospital administrator has notified the police. We're doing everything we can to locate him."

Suddenly a thought occurred to me and I turned to Dave. "Let's call home."

The idea seemed like a good one, but got us nowhere. Kallie had neither seen nor heard from Joshua. Confident that the entire hospital had been thoroughly searched, Dave and I raced to our car and drove through the dimly lit streets of town. We searched all night, everywhere we thought Joshua might be. We even called the county morgue. But our search was in vain. There was no sign of him, anywhere.

The following night was Christmas Eve. We gathered as a family around the tree, as was our custom, yet none of us felt much like celebrating. Our thoughts and concerns were naturally focused on Joshua. The police called every few hours, but had nothing to report.

I lay in bed that night thinking of Joshua, wondering what had happened to my dear friend. The house felt lonely without him. I missed his smile. I missed his laughter. I missed the way I felt whenever I was with him. We all did.

I arose early Christmas morning, prepared a cup of cinnamon tea and made my way to Emily's room. I guess it served as a haven for me in Joshua's absence. I stared out the window into the darkness. A light Christmas snow was falling softly to the ground. I could see the tiny flakes as they passed through the glow of the streetlight from across the road. So many unanswered questions raced through my mind. Who was Joshua? Why had he come into my life? Where was he now? I lowered my head in frustration. The pieces just wouldn't fit together.

An hour or so later I heard Dave and the children enter the family room. I turned to join them and out of the corner of my eye noticed something lying on Emily's pillow. Curious, I walked closer. A Christmas present, the size of a large jewelry box, together with a card, lay nestled in the quilt that covered her bed. I opened the card and immediately recognized the unsteady handwriting; it was Joshua's. My entire body trembled as I opened the card and began to read:

Mrs. Andersen, I am most certain that you have by now exhausted every effort in an attempt to find me, and have concerned yourself with my well-being. For I know that you have loved me as I have loved you. Fear not, dear lady, and worry no more. All is well.

Merry Christmas, Mrs. Andersen, and may God bless you and your wonderful family. Until we meet again. Love, Joshua.

Dazed, I lowered myself onto Emily's bed, trying to make sense of it all. After a moment, my attention was drawn back to the gift. Perhaps what lay inside would dispel the confusion I felt. At least that was my hope.

I untied the green ribbon, removed the wrapping paper, lifted the cover and peered inside. It was a necklace. Removing it from its container, to my amazement I held in my hand an ancient gold medallion.

I shook my head in disbelief as I examined the intricate charm, trying to convince myself that the precious object was not what I knew it to be. It couldn't be; that was impossible. But it was. Somehow, some way, it was.

I closed my eyes and thought of the old man, as I clutched the medallion to my chest. The events of the last few weeks passed before me as if in slow motion, causing my body to quiver as revelations of understanding flooded my mind. Suddenly, it all made perfect sense.

Joshua had once claimed that I saved his life after feeding him a simple bowl of soup. But in truth it was he who had come to save me. Who better to teach me the miracle I so desperately needed to understand?

I've heard it said that time heals all wounds. There might be some truth to that, but my heart never truly began to mend until I met Joshua. I'm not saying it's easy. It's not. Anyone who's ever lost a child knows that. I still miss Emily and Jenny terribly. I think I always will. And every so often, in the quiet moments of the day, I shed tears when tender memories return. But I'm no longer racked by tragic nightmares of Emily's death. Miraculously, they have given way to peaceful dreams of a glorious reunion.

I yearn for that day. I can imagine nothing sweeter than to embrace my little girls, to hold them, to love them, never to be separated again.

I need only be patient. Such a day will come. Of this I have no doubt, for the little girl I saw in my dream that night was Emily, and the man who so tenderly held her close had nail prints in his hands.

Such is the Miracle of Christmas, and there is none greater in all the world. For it is a miracle wrought in love. A perfect love. A divine love. A precious gift bestowed on each of us that first Christmas night in a small village so very long ago.

It's the miracle Joshua came to teach me. The miracle he wanted me to share.

For me, Christmas will never be the same – and for that I give thanks.

"Mom, Mom, come quick," screamed Kallie as she skipped into the room and grasped my hand.

"What is it, Sweetheart?" I asked as I was pulled down the hall.

When we entered the family room, she pointed toward the top of the tree, exclaiming, "Look!"

I gazed upward, and through my tears saw, not the lighted star that normally graced our tree, but rather two small porcelain angels. They stood side by side, as if holding hands, watching over each other, caring for each other. I smiled and looked heavenward.

I'm sure they are.